Adapted by Stephanie Calmenson

Cover illustration by Denise Shimabukuro and Brent Ford

Illustrated by Francesc Mateu

A Random House PICTUREBACK® Book

Random House 🏠 New York

Copyright © 1997, 2003 Disney Enterprises, Inc. All rights reserved under International and Pan-American Copyright Conventions. Published in the United States by Random House Children's Books, a division of Random House, Inc., New York, and simultaneously in Canada by Random House of Canada Limited, Toronto, in conjunction with Disney Enterprises, Inc. Originally published in slightly different form by Golden Books in 1997.
Library of Congress Control Number: 2002107543
ISBN: 0-7364-2128-9
www.randomhouse.com/kids/disney
First Random House Edition 2003
Printed in the United States of America   20 19 18
PICTUREBACK, RANDOM HOUSE, and the Random House colophon are registered trademarks of Random House, Inc.

Sebastian, the court composer, had planned a royal concert. It was in honor of Triton, the sea king, and all his daughters were to sing. But Ariel, the daughter with the most beautiful voice, hadn't shown up.

Triton was losing his patience. "ARIEL!" he called.

Ariel could not hear her father. She was busy exploring a sunken ship. The Little Mermaid wanted to know all she could about the creatures called humans.

"Oh, my gosh!" Ariel cried. She held up a fork. "Have you ever seen anything so wonderful in your life?"

"But what is it?" asked her friend Flounder.

Ariel and Flounder went to ask Scuttle the seagull. They found him perched on his favorite rock.

"It's a dinglehopper," he said with certainty. "Humans use these little babies to straighten their hair."

Ariel was fascinated. Now she knew one more thing about humans.

Later that day, Ariel was human-watching. She spotted a handsome young man on a ship. As soon as Ariel laid eyes on Prince Eric, she fell in love.

But soon a storm began to rage.

The ship was in trouble!

Prince Eric was trying to steer through the storm when a bolt of lightning flashed. The ship's sail caught fire. Rough waves tossed the ship back and forth. Eric went flying into the sea.

"I must save him!" cried Ariel. She dove underwater and pulled the prince safely ashore.

Prince Eric was very still for a very long time. Scuttle wasn't sure if he was alive. But suddenly Ariel saw his chest move. Up and down. Up and down.

"Look, he's breathing!" Ariel cried. She began to sing a love song to him but was soon interrupted by Prince Eric's dog, Max.

Ariel hurried back into the water. With Flounder by her side, she headed for home.

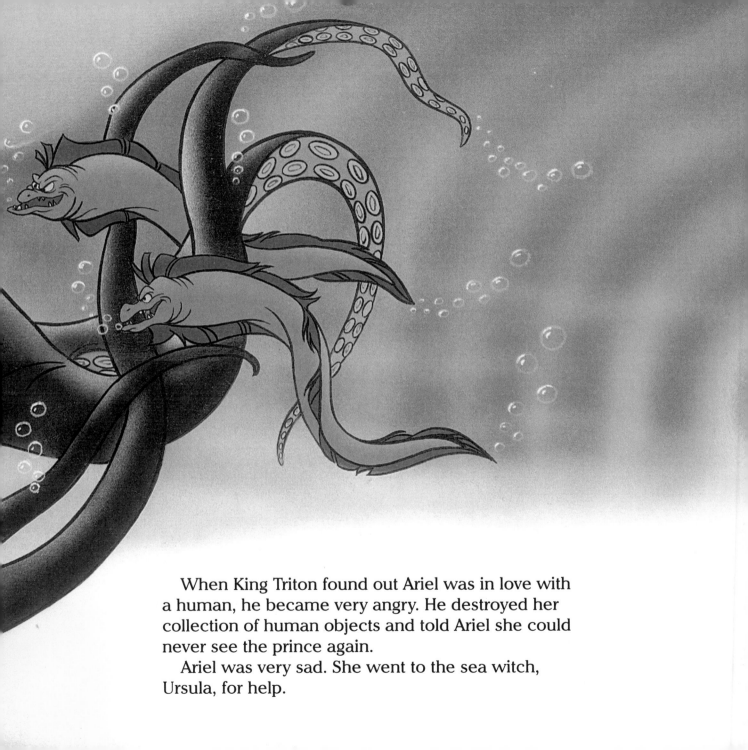

When King Triton found out Ariel was in love with a human, he became very angry. He destroyed her collection of human objects and told Ariel she could never see the prince again.

Ariel was very sad. She went to the sea witch, Ursula, for help.

"The only way to get what you want is to become human," Ursula explained.

The plan sounded simple enough. Ursula would turn Ariel into a human for three days. If Ariel could get the prince to kiss her, she would remain human forever. If not, she would turn back into a mermaid—and belong to Ursula.

But there was a price for Ursula's magic. "What I want from you is your voice!" the evil sea witch demanded.

Because she was in love, Ariel agreed.

With a swirl of her magic potion, Ursula took away Ariel's voice and dropped it into a seashell locket.

Ariel looked down where her tail used to be. She had legs! Flounder quickly swam her up to the surface.

Prince Eric had recovered nicely by the time Flounder dragged Ariel to shore. When the prince saw Ariel, he did not know that she was the one who had saved him. Without her voice, Ariel couldn't sing to him or tell him who she was.

But Prince Eric liked Ariel very much. He took her rowing at twilight. Triton had asked Sebastian to watch over Ariel, so the crab tried to help things along. He led Scuttle and his friends in a romantic song.

"Kiss the girl!" they sang.

But the prince did not kiss Ariel. Not on the first day, nor on the second.

On the third day, Scuttle surprised Ariel with the news
that Prince Eric was getting married. On board the wedding
ship, everyone was busy getting ready, including Vanessa,
the bride-to-be, who was singing happily.

Scuttle heard her beautiful voice and flew down to the ship.
Looking through a porthole, he saw Vanessa look in a mirror.

"It's the sea witch!" cried Scuttle. He flew off for help as
quickly as he could.

In no time, sea creatures and birds rushed the ship and began to attack Vanessa.

Vanessa's seashell locket crashed to the deck. It opened, freeing Ariel's voice just as she pulled herself aboard.

The prince heard Ariel speak, and at last, he knew that Ariel was the one who had rescued him. He went to kiss her, but the sun had set. Ariel's three days were up.

"You're too late!" screamed Ursula.

"We made a deal!" Ursula said. The sea witch grabbed
Ariel and dove into the sea.
    When they reached the ocean floor, King Triton appeared.
"Let her go!" he demanded.

"I might be willing to make an exchange for someone even better," Ursula said slyly.

King Triton sadly agreed to the sea witch's deal. Ariel was set free, and Triton allowed himself to be turned into a lowly sea creature.

"Now I am the ruler of all the ocean!" shouted Ursula.

Soon Ursula found herself face to face with Prince Eric,
who had come to rescue Ariel.
    They battled above and below the sea.
    Finally, Eric killed wicked Ursula. Triton was the sea king
once more.

"She really does love him, doesn't she?" Triton asked Sebastian.
The crab assured the king that Ariel belonged with the prince.
With a wave of his trident, Triton turned Ariel into a human being.

It wasn't long before Prince Eric and Ariel were married. All
the creatures of the sea and land were there to congratulate the
happy couple.